The Wish Cat

Ragnhild Scamell

illustrated by **Gaby Hansen**

LITTLE TIGER PRESS

This Little Tiger book belongs to:

_____

_____

_____

_____

To Thomas James, with love
~ RS
For Mum and Dad
~ GH

LITTLE TIGER PRESS
An imprint of Magi Publications
1 The Coda Centre, 189 Munster Road, London SW6 6AW, UK
www.littletigerpress.com
First published in Great Britain 2001
by Little Tiger Press, London
This edition published in 2008
Text copyright © 2001 Ragnhild Scamell
Illustrations copyright © 2001 Gaby Hansen
Ragnhild Scamell and Gaby Hansen have asserted their rights
to be identified as the author and illustrator of this work
under the Copyright, Designs and Patents Act, 1988.
All rights reserved
ISBN 978-1-84506-893-6
Printed in China
3 5 7 9 10 8 6 4

Holly's house had a cat flap.
It was a small door in the big
door so a cat could come and go.

But Holly didn't have a cat.

One night, something magical
happened. Holly saw a falling star.
As the star trailed across the sky, she
made a wish.

"I wish I had a kitten," she whispered.
"A tiny cuddly kitten who could jump
in and out of the cat flap."

CRASH!

Something big landed on the windowsill outside.

It wasn't a kitten . . .

It was Tom, the scruffiest, most raggedy cat Holly had ever seen. He sat there in the moonlight, smiling a crooked smile.

"Meo-o-ow!"

"I'm Tom, your wish cat," he seemed to say.

"It's a mistake," cried Holly.
"I wished for a kitten."
Tom didn't think Holly had
made a mistake.

He rubbed his torn ear
against the window and
howled so loudly it made
him cough and splutter.

"Meo-o-ow, o-o-w, o-o-w!"

Holly hid under her
covers, hoping that
he'd go away.

The next morning, Tom was still there, waiting for her outside the cat flap. He wanted to come in, and he had brought her a present of a smelly old piece of fish.

"Yuck!" said Holly. She picked it up and dropped it in the garbage can. Tom looked puzzled.
"Bad cat," she said, shooing him away.

"Go on, go home!" said Holly, walking over to her swing.

But Tom was there before her. He sharpened his claws on the swing . . .

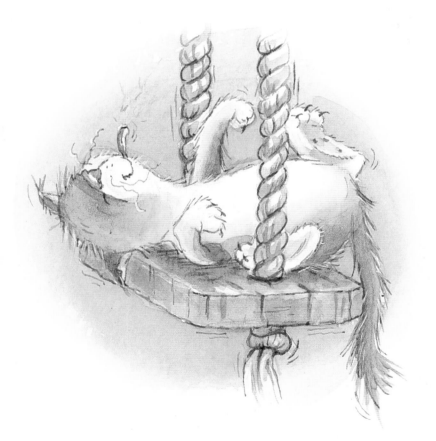

and washed his coat noisily, pulling out bits of fur and spitting them everywhere.

At lunchtime, Tom sat on the
windowsill, watching Holly eat.

She broke off a piece of her sandwich and passed it out to him through the cat flap. Tom wolfed it down, purring all the time.

In the afternoon, a cold wind swept through the garden, and Holly had to wear her jacket and scarf. Tom didn't seem to feel the cold. He followed her around . . .

chasing leaves . . .

balancing on top of
the fence . . .

showing off.

Soon it was time for Holly
to go inside.
"Bye, Tom," she said, and
stroked his scruffy head.

Tom followed her to the door and
settled himself by the cat flap.

That evening, it snowed.
Sparkly flakes of snow
danced in the air.
Outside the cat flap,
Tom curled himself into a
ragged ball to keep warm.
Soon there was a white
cushion of snow all over
the doorstep, and on Tom.

Holly heard him meowing
miserably. She ran to the
cat flap and held it open.

Tom came in, shaking snow all over the
kitchen floor.
"Poor old Tom," said Holly.

He ate a large plate of food, and drank an
even larger bowl of warm milk.
Tom purred louder than ever when Holly
dried him with the kitchen towel.

Soon Tom had settled down,
snug on Holly's bed.
Holly stroked his scruffy fur,
and together they watched
the glittering stars.

Then, suddenly, another star
fell. Holly couldn't think of
a single thing to wish for.
She had everything she
wanted. And so had Tom.

Fantastic reads from Little Tiger Press

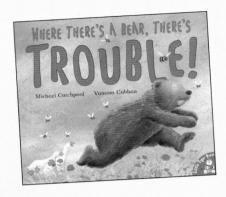

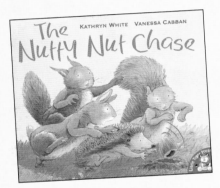

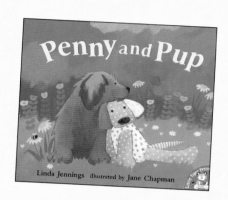

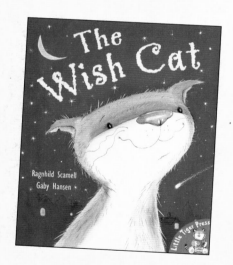

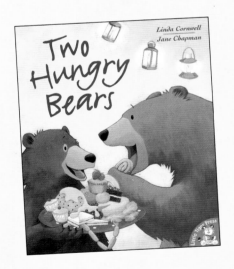

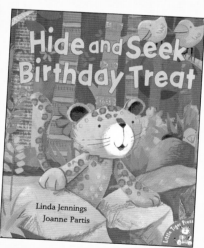

For information regarding any of the above titles
or for our catalogue, please contact us:
Little Tiger Press, 1 The Coda Centre,
189 Munster Road, London SW6 6AW, UK
Tel: +44 (0)20 7385 6333 Fax: +44 (0)20 7385 7333
E-mail: info@littletiger.co.uk
www.littletigerpress.com